THIS WALKER BOOK BELONGS TO:

For the children of
Appledore School
A.B.

For my mother
C.M.

First published 1987 by
Walker Books Ltd
87 Vauxhall Walk
London SE11 5HJ

This edition published 1990

Text © 1987 Barbara Anthony
Illustrations © 1987 Claudio Munoz

Printed and bound in Italy by
L.E.G.O., Vicenza

British Library Cataloguing in Publication Data
Barber, Antonia
Satchelmouse and the dolls' house.
Rn: Barbara Anthony I. Title II. Munoz, Claudio
823'.914 [J]   PZ7
ISBN 0-7445-1454-1

Satchelmouse

and

THE DOLL'S HOUSE

Written by Antonia Barber

Illustrated by Claudio Muñoz

WALKER BOOKS
LONDON

The village school had a big doll's house.

It had once belonged to an old lady who lived nearby.

The old lady had played with it when she was a little girl.

Sarah thought the doll's house was beautiful.

She liked the four-poster bed with its pink silk covers.

She liked the pretty curving staircase with the red carpet.

She liked the tiny china plates on the dining-room table.

She liked the shiny black stove in the basement kitchen.

The doll's house had a family of dolls who lived upstairs.

The family had a lot of servants who lived downstairs.

"Which of the dolls would you like to be?" Mrs James asked the children.

"I'd like to be the father," said Darren. The father had side-whiskers and looked very important.

"I want to be the cook," said Jenny, who liked to play with the tiny pots and pans.

"I'd be the butler," said Mark, "and taste all the lovely food."

"I'd like to be the little girl," said Sarah.

The little girl had rosy cheeks and a white frock. She sat at a frilly dressing table. She slept in the four-poster bed.

Sarah's friend Satchelmouse was listening. He was a tall brown mouse in a red jacket. Inside the jacket was a useful pencil case. Satchelmouse carried a golden trumpet. It looked like a pencil sharpener, but Sarah knew that it had magic powers.

"Do you really want to be the little girl?" asked Satchelmouse.

"Oh, yes, please!" said Sarah. She was looking at the rosebuds on the white frock.

She did not notice that Satchelmouse was smiling to himself.

He picked up the magic trumpet and began to play.

Sarah grew smaller and smaller.
She found herself in the pretty bedroom standing beside the four-poster bed.
She hurried over to the dressing table to look at herself in the mirror…but she saw to her horror that she was a little *servant* girl in a mobcap and apron!

The bedroom door flew open and in came
the girl in the white frock.

Her rosy face looked very bad tempered.
"Stop admiring yourself in my mirror,"
she told Sarah crossly, "and make my bed."
Making a four-poster bed was not easy.
Sarah was quite out of breath when
she had finished.

"Now get back below stairs,
where you belong," said the doll
in the white frock.

As Sarah went down the pretty
curving staircase, she met
the father coming up.
  "This carpet is very dusty!"
he said. "Clean it at once!"
  It took a long time to brush
the red carpet. Sarah grew
hot and dirty.

"This is all your fault, Satchelmouse,"
she protested. "You knew I wanted
to be the girl in the white frock."
"You only said 'the little girl',"
Satchelmouse pointed out.
"But I didn't even notice the little
servant girl," explained Sarah.
"Nobody ever does," said Satchelmouse.

The butler came out of the dining room with a tray of dirty plates. "Take these to the kitchen," he said, "and wash them up."

When Sarah had finished the plates, the butler brought more dirty dishes.

By the time they were all done, Sarah felt tired and greasy.

The cook came bustling in.
"If you've finished washing up, you
can polish the stove," she said.
    When Sarah complained, the cook
chased her around the kitchen
with a rolling pin.

It took so long to make the stove clean and shiny. Sarah's face and hands were covered with black polish.

"Magic me back to the classroom, Satchelmouse," she begged, "before they find me any more work to do!"

"Poor Sarah," said Satchelmouse, trying hard not to laugh.

He played her a cheerful tune and she began to grow again.

Soon she was back outside the doll's house, looking in.

Sarah found the little servant doll behind the table in the kitchen.

She was out of sight, scrubbing the floor.

When no one was looking, Sarah took off the doll's cap and apron and dressed her in the white frock.

She laid her on the four-poster bed.

"You need a good rest!" she told her.

Then Sarah dressed the rosy-cheeked doll
in the cap and apron and put her
in the kitchen.

"See how *you* like it!" she said.

MORE WALKER PAPERBACKS
For You to Enjoy

SATCHELMOUSE AND THE DOLL'S HOUSE
by Antonia Barber/Claudio Muñoz

Another magical Satchelmouse adventure. This time, Satchelmouse
turns Sarah into a servant girl in her own doll's house!

ISBN 0-7445-1454-1 £2.99

QUACK QUACK
CLUCK CLUCK
by Patricia Casey

Two colourful farmyard tales. In *Quack Quack* a duck and
a hen have an argument over some eggs, while in *Cluck Cluck* a
dog tries to save the farmer's hens from a hungry fox.

"Delightful... Patricia Casey's washes are full of animation. They make full
use of natural forms as well as the humour and drama in the situation.
There is no age limit to this fun." *The Junior Bookshelf*

ISBN 0-7445-1425-8 *Quack Quack*
ISBN 0-7445-1426-6 *Cluck Cluck*
£2.99 each

**Walker Paperbacks are available from most booksellers, or by post from
Walker Books Ltd, PO Box 11, Falmouth, Cornwall TR10 9EN**

To order, send:
Title, author, ISBN number and price for each book ordered
Your full name and address
Cheque or postal order for the total amount, plus postage and packing:

UK, BFPO and Eire – 50p for first book, plus 10p for
each additional book to a maximum charge of £2.00.
Overseas Customers – £1.25 for first book,
plus 25p per copy for each additional book.

Prices are correct at time of going to press but are subject to change without notice.